Something Rotten

Katie Penryn grew up in Kenya. Her father was the Commercial Officer for the British High Commission in Mombasa. The setting for the stories is Mazita, a fictional island off the coast of Opunto, itself a fictional East African country. Although Katie's stories about Bob Dukes and his three children, Poppy, Suze and Charlie are pure invention, the reader soon realizes that Katie has drawn heavily on her loving memories of a magic childhood. Nevertheless, with a gentle smile, she sends up the political and social life of the times.

By the same author and available from Amazon.com and other book stores

<u>Our Man in Mazita</u>

Beau—ootiful Soo—oop!
Something Spotted
Christmas in Mazita

<u>Katie's Tales</u>

The Lobster's Tale

SOMETHING ROTTEN

(Lobster Mobster)

KATIE PENRYN

 Karibu Publishers

Something Rotten

Published in the United States by
Karibu Publishers

Printed by CreateSpace

Ebook : ASIN: B00AQFD9J8

Paperback : ISBN-13:978-1494957490
ISBN-10:1494957493

TABLE OF CONTENTS

"Something is rotten in the state of
Denmark."

Hamlet

William Shakespeare

Chapter 1 — Development Plans

BOB DUKES, COMMERCIAL OFFICER AND AIDE TO THE GOVERNOR OF MAZITA, heard the sound of the advance motorcycle escort long before the motorcade reached him. He pulled over to the side of the road, onto a dusty patch of ground beneath a large flamboyant tree, and closed the car windows against the inevitable dust cloud.

It could only be the President of Opunto. It didn't pay to hinder his progress for his vanguard were well-known for their thuggish behavior. Seconds later, the cavalcade passed him at a rush, horns blaring, lights flashing. A Silver Cloud Rolls Royce with its top speed of over 100 miles an hour. Yes, it was Mzee

Jefferson Jambo; his pennant snapping in the breeze.

Opunto, mainland neighbor of the island of Mazita on the East African coast, had recently achieved independence. Mazita, itself, had been hived off Opunto and created as a Crown protectorate and off-shore financial center.

Jefferson Jambo coming to see the Governor of Mazita? Why? Bob would have been notified in the normal course of business of any impending formal visit. So it had to be unscheduled.

The Rolls came to a halt beneath the porte cochère as Bob drew up for the security checks at the gates to Government House. Two people stepped out of the car. Bob didn't recognize the tall, slim visitor who took the steps two at a time, leaving the much shorter President to follow on behind.

Bob acknowledged the *askari*'s salute and drove round to the side of Government House.

He had barely had time to settle down in his office with its view out over the Indian Ocean, when he heard a knock at the door and an excited Sir Phillip hurried in.

"Bob, will you come to my office at once, please. There's someone I'd like you to meet."

"I saw the car arrive, Sir. I gather Mzee Jefferson Jambo has called on you."

"Yes, JJ's here but it's his visitor I want you to meet. Come along, hurry it up," said Sir Phillip, trying to shoo Bob out of the office. "This can't wait all day. We have to move fast on this one."

Bob's first impression of the visitor was one of elegance. He wore a well-cut white linen tropical suit. He had a sharply planed face with high cheek bones and ebony colored hair swept back off his face. The sketch of a moustache traced a line above full lips. He nodded at Bob and waited for the introductions.

Bob walked forward to greet the President first. JJ shook his hand with unexpected gusto.

"Let me introduce you to my friend, Mr. Giuseppe Nolini," said JJ turning towards the visitor. "We met at Harvard. You remember my time there on a US scholarship?"

"Oh, you're an American?" asked Bob, offering his hand.

"No, I'm Sicilian," answered Nolini, as he stepped forward to shake Bob's. "I spent time in the States to further my education – just like JJ."

"And the name 'Nolini'? Are you related to Annette and Johnny Nolini by any chance?"

The name had piqued Bob's curiosity because Annette Nolini was his daughter Suze's music teacher. Her husband, Johnny, worked as an aircraft mechanic for Alitalia, Italy's flagship airline.

"Very distantly," replied Nolini with a smile. A smile which didn't quite reach his eyes. "Johnny's family left Sicily for Milan just after the war and we lost touch, but I look forward to seeing him again."

"That's enough chitchat," interrupted the Governor. "Come, let's all sit down and discuss what brought you here today. JJ –, Mr. Nolini—"

"Oh, please call me Joe," said the visitor, pulling out a chair and seating himself well back from the table, with an ankle resting on the other knee. Bob thought his informality smacked of disrespect to the Governor, but Sir Phillip didn't appear to mind.

"Bob, order up some coffee, will you?" said Sir Phillip, sitting down at the head of the conference table.

Once the coffee arrived the meeting got down to business.

JJ explained that Nolini had come forward with a project which would be beneficial to the island of Mazita. Nolini came from a wealthy family who wanted to invest in Mazita's new status as an off-shore base.

Nolini himself expanded on the idea. "We would like to build an up-market hotel and casino here on the island. Our research has shown that, although your hotels here on the island are charming, they don't have the modern facilities that richer clients expect."

"Such as?" responded Bob in a defensive tone.

"There is no air conditioning. En suite bathrooms are rare. The décor is worn. Some of hotels are frankly just shabby. And none of the hotels on the island has a swimming pool, let alone a casino."

"They've been good enough for our visitors up till now. And what do you want a swimming pool for when you can drive off the island to the mainland and swim off the best beaches in the world?" argued Bob.

"Modern travelers want the convenience of a pool as part of the hotel complex, Bob."

JJ jumped into the argument. "Bob, with independence and all the money that's flowing into Opunto and Mazita, our tourist industry is getting a tremendous boost. I understand holiday makers and businessmen are becoming more sophisticated. The hard postwar years of the fifties are a thing of the past. Economists are predicting a period of expansion and boom for the sixties. Both countries need to be poised to take advantage of this."

"What do you think, Sir?" asked Bob turning to the Governor.

"I've been consulting with the Foreign and Commonwealth Office and their opinion is that there is a market here for a casino and five-star hotel. They point out that there is a rapidly growing African middle class in the newly independent countries. And we can tap into the white market of the puritanical countries in southern Africa where gambling is illegal, like South Africa."

Bob reflected for a moment. "I do agree we need a hotel with modern facilities here on the island for all our business visitors. But why a casino?"

Well, Bob," said Nolini. "That's the icing on the cake. Mazita does have a major competitor as an off-shore banking centre - the Cayman Islands. But the Caymans have made it quite clear that they will never allow gambling on their islands. That leaves the field clear for Mazita. The perfect combination: a casino and off-shore banking."

Bob didn't look convinced but then he didn't have to be. He didn't have any executive powers. His role was advisory at best. "So where do I fit in, Sir?" he asked turning to the Governor.

"I'd like you to set up a meeting between John Richardson, the Managing Director of the Commercial and International Bank here in Mazita, and Mr. Nolini ... Joe ... to thrash out the financial ramifications of all this and see if it is feasible."

"What about the site for the hotel and casino, Joe? Have you anywhere in mind?" asked Bob.

"We've done some preliminary research, but I would like you to arrange a meeting with the Town Clerk so that we can discuss the availability of the land and the provision of services," added Joe Nolini. "And with any local labor leaders. Our demand for labor is going to be quite significant. The development will provide employment for the building sector during the construction, and then for hotel and casino staff once the new complex is ready for business."

"All of which would be good for Mazita," agreed Bob. "Right, I'll see to all that. Are we all to meet back here to discuss the plans before you make a decision, Sir Phillip?"

"Bob, I've already given my permission in principle on condition that the CI Bank and the Town Council have no objections. I suggest we meet to finalize the project as soon as Joe has all the assurances he needs to continue with the development. Agreed?"

Everyone nodded and Bob returned to his office to seek counsel from his friend, the Queen.

Chapter 2 – Her Majesty's Warning

WHEN THE OFFICE WAS FIRST ALLOCATED TO HIM, Bob had been pleased to notice that a copy of Annigoni's painting of the Queen hung on the wall. The artist had made this likeness during the first years of her reign. It showed Her Majesty, dressed in the robes of the Order of the Garter, standing against a Renaissance background.

Bob had felt an immediate sense of identity with the Queen, as both he and Her Majesty faced overwhelming difficulties in their respective positions. The young Queen was to take on the leadership of a country still recovering from the ravages of the Second

World War, together with the responsibility of steering a disintegrating empire into a new commonwealth of nations. Bob had recently assumed the role of single parent to his three children, twelve-year old Poppy, eight-year old Suze and their younger brother, Charlie. In addition, he didn't feel confident in his appointment as Commercial Officer, considering himself neither adequate nor qualified.

The first time he heard the Queen speak to him he thought he was hearing things … going mad, perhaps. Over time he had learned to accept the phenomenon and enjoy his conversations with Her Majesty for she had a dry sense of humor and a vast fund of knowledge at her command.

Bob walked up to the portrait to see if the Queen felt like talking as she didn't always. "You'll never guess what I've just been told, Your Majesty," he began.

The Queen's gaze came to life and her eyes sought his face. "No, Mr Dukes. Pray do tell. What have you just been told?"

Bob explained the proposed project of setting up a hotel and casino on the island.

"I detect a note of skepticism or anxiety in your voice, Mr Dukes. What are you worried about?"

"First of all, Ma'am, this whole idea has come out of the blue. It doesn't seem to have received much serious consideration. And ... well... I didn't much take to this Nolini character. Yes, he's good looking, though perhaps a bit too much so. Sartorially savvy and charming on the surface. But there's something off. His handshake is just a touch reptilian."

"You mean he's a cold fish?"

"No, it's not quite that. He exudes bonhomie but I think it's fake, Ma'am."

"I know from my morning briefings from the Prime Minister that Number Ten have looked into the backers for this scheme and everything seems to be above board. Mind you, Mr Dukes, I always do find it hard to take handsome men at face value. That's all good looks are, after all, face value."

"And this one will make us a magnet for tourism and business investment and give us the opportunity to raise our profile in the world. He appears to be bringing so much to our table: employment and a modern hotel/casino complex."

"You mean you think it's all just a little too good to be true, Mr Dukes?"

"Something like that. I feel uneasy about him but it's just me. The Governor and JJ think he's wonderful."

"You remind me of an incident buried somewhere in my classical education – something to do with the Trojan War."

"Ah, you mean the Wooden Horse, Ma'am?"

"Exactly, Mr Dukes. How does it go? *Timeo Danaos et dona ferentes.*"

"Meaning, Ma'am?"

"*I fear the Greeks even when they bear gifts.*"

"But the Greeks and the Trojans were enemies. The Italians aren't our enemies. They've been our allies since the end of the war, Ma'am."

The Queen looked at Bob thoughtfully. "The Italians, yes. But can one say the same for the Sicilians?"

"So you think I should keep my eyes open, Ma'am?"

"Yes, I do, Mr Dukes. I do indeed. I wouldn't want something untoward to sabotage the success of the island of Mazita. It's an asset of great importance to my Government."

Chapter 3 — Nolini and his Hotel

A FORTNIGHT LATER THE GOVERNOR CALLED for a follow-up meeting between the interested parties. Nolini announced that a suitable site had been found on the headland on the south side of the island. Situated on hitherto protected wasteland, the site overlooked the entrance to the creek which ran in from the Indian Ocean and separated the island from the southern mainland. This creek led to the deep water harbor in the port of Kalindi. All the large oceangoing vessels would have to pass the hotel complex on their way inwards to their berths, which would make for interesting viewing for the guests.

This news surprised Bob as he had understood that the land had been kept undeveloped in order to give all the islanders unhindered access to the seafront. He wondered how what he would have thought were obvious objections to the scheme had been overcome, but he didn't say anything as his role was only that of secretary to the meeting.

The CI Bank would advance the financing for the project. This was unexpected, too. Bob had thought that Nolini's family would be providing the investment. When he queried this point in order to clarifiy his note-taking, the Governor told him that the Nolini family would indeed be investing large sums in Mazita's development, but that they were depositing the funds with the bank. It was up to the bank to decide what investments to undertake. They had determined to back the casino development with long term loans secured on the property and land.

All present agreed in favor of the project. The Governor signed his official approval and set the ground-breaking ceremony for that week. Now the decision had been taken, everyone involved wanted to hurry the plan along as fast as possible with a view to a Christmas opening – Christmas being the height of the tourist season on the East African coast.

Hotel *Mahali Mzuri* or Hotel Splendid - literally 'the Good Place' - would soon be in operation.

THE BUILDING SITE, Government House and the children's primary school were three points of a triangle. Bob and the children regularly stopped off at the site on the way home so that Bob could keep an unofficial eye on progress. Poppy, Suze and Charlie, like most children, were fascinated by the construction work. Charlie especially liked to watch the JCB's and the cement delivery trucks doing their work. He planned to be a heavy plant operator when he grew up, he said. As the floors rose the children ran about playing tag or hide and seek, jumping up and down the half-finished staircases and tearing round the concrete support columns.

Joe Nolini visited the site often to crack the whip, making sure that the Clerk of Works knew his job and that the Architect signed off on the planned phases according to schedule.

Poppy and Suze were smitten with Joe. Tall, handsome, always ready with a flattering remark, he could do no wrong. Young as they were, the girls were susceptible to his charm.

But Charlie wasn't. Bob noticed that Charlie hung back whenever Joe appeared and began a conversation. At first, Bob thought Charlie was just shy, but eventually he had to admit to himself that Charlie just didn't like Joe. Maybe like himself, Charlie thought Joe had more smarm than charm.

Annette Nolini was also a fan of Joe's. She never failed to mention him when she and Bob chatted at the end of Suze's weekly piano lesson. Bob supposed that only natural. After all, with Joe Nolini being a distant cousin of Annette's husband, they must be seeing each other frequently.

Bob learned that Annette's father, Dominique LaGrange, who had a small holding on the northern mainland and who was something of a fishing expert, had been taking Joe Nolini out with him in his fishing boat and teaching him about deep sea fishing.

Annette added with a wink that that was not all her father was teaching Joe. Bob didn't understand the joke but, not wanting to admit that he didn't, he smiled as if he did.

AT LONG LAST THE HOTEL WAS READY for its grand opening. It stood proudly on the headland. Its four stories made it the tallest building on the island. The rooms were furnished with panache. Each had a balcony looking out over the entrance to the creek and then onwards to the horizon out on the Indian Ocean.

The likes of the swimming pool and the ballroom had never been seen on the East African coast. With its luxurious and temptingly wicked casino, the hotel had attracted advance bookings greater than forecast. The project was set to be a success before it even opened its doors.

On the day before the opening ceremony Bob was coaxing his reluctant children to tidy up their room ready for the Christmas celebrations. In addition to their bedroom, Poppy, Suze and Charlie had gradually colonized the large verandah which ran all the way round their old wooden house. Not particularly tidy by nature himself, Bob realized that he had not been setting a good example to the children. Peter, their Swahili housekeeper, had complained to Bob that it was impossible for him to keep the house clean when it was so cluttered. Bob had to admit that Peter had a point: three dogs and three unruly children did make for a heavy workload.

"Now, you three, listen up. There'll be no Christmas Tree until this place is spick and span."

"But it's so hot, Daddy," complained Suze. "Can't we leave it till later?" she added, flopping down on the floor with her arms round Lobo's neck. Poor old Lobo, Suze's black German Shepherd, was already panting.

"Yes, Daddy, can't we do it tomorrow?" added Charlie.

"You know very well that if I let you off today, tomorrow will never come. I know tidying up is boring but it has to be done. We won't enjoy the holidays if everything around us is in a mess."

"Oh, all right then," said Poppy, giving in and starting to dismantle a den the children had built at the end of the verandah. Even Poppy, who was usually her father's little helper, was disgruntled at having to work in the tropical heat and high humidity of the East African coast at Christmastime.

Bob left the children to their chores and went to tidy his own room. At times like these he realized just how much his estranged wife had done to keep their children and their home clean and tidy. It was possible that the children missed having a sense of discipline and order in their young lives. He could never get the balance right; one moment persuasive, the next authoritarian. Children needed consistency. But he couldn't turn the clock back.

The sound of a vehicle drawing up outside broke into his self-deprecating thoughts.

A horn tooted, *"Shave and a haircut, two bits."* Then a car door slammed.

Bob put down the clothes he was folding and looked out of the window. The children were already rushing down the steps to the garden, followed by three barking dogs.

It was Joe Nolini of all people. Standing in front of a large station wagon. Beaming with another one of his false smiles. Charlie hung back but the girls were dancing up and down in front of Joe, showing off for all they were worth.

"Hello, Joe! What are you doing here?" they giggled and preened while the dogs jumped about barking and yapping with excitement.

"For Pete's sake, girls, give the man some room," Bob shouted down to them. How could they be so embarrassing? And he turned to walk quickly down the steps to find out why Nolini was calling on them without warning.

"Hey, Bob," Nolini greeted him. "I've brought something for your kids for Christmas."

"Oh yes?"

"Don't look so dismayed. I wanted to give them all a present for being such good kids."

Bob felt Charlie's hand seek his. "Oh, we really couldn't accept, Joe."

"Daddy!" cried Poppy and Suze together. "Please!"

"Bob, it's Christmas. Don't be such a misery."

"Well, I suppose it won't do them any harm. Let's have a look then."

Nolini went round to the rear of the vehicle and the children followed him closely trying to see into the back. He opened the hatch and pulled a piece of tarpaulin off ... three brand new bicycles!

That was the end of Bob's attempts to refuse Nolini's gifts. Once the children saw that the bikes had three-gears, he had no chance. Even Charlie appeared to be won over. At least he shook Nolini's hand with adult solemnity. Bob in his turn thanked Nolini with as good a grace as he could summon, but privately he still reserved judgment about the man.

Chapter 4 – First Rumblings

PETER WAS PLEASED to find that the children had tidied up the house when he returned to work next morning. "*Asante sana,*" he told them.

The children wasted no time showing him their new treasures. Peter who had only an old black Raleigh sit-up-and-beg bicycle to ride to and from work – no gears - was impressed with their gifts, but he obviously wondered why someone unrelated to them had given the children such expensive presents. He and Bob discussed the matter while Peter prepared the lunch.

"This Mr Nolini, he's the boss of the hotel, *Mahali Mzuri?*" Peter asked Bob.

"Yes, that's right. He's an important businessman who is bringing employment to Mazita."

"Is that what they say up at Government House, *Bwana*?"

"Why? What do you know that's different?" asked Bob noticing Peter's sarcastic tone which was surprising for someone usually so polite.

"Perhaps you should know, *Bwana*, that we locals call the hotel *Mahali Mbaya*, not *Mahali Mzuri*."

"*Mbaya*? You mean 'bad'? You call it *Mahali Mbaya*, the 'bad place'?"

"Yes, *Bwana*."

"But why?"

"I have a cousin who worked there on the construction site. He tells stories of intimidation. The laborers had to pay their bosses a cut of their wages and the hotel workers have to do the same now."

"But that's normal practice here in Africa, isn't it, Peter?" asked Bob.

"Yes, it is. But this is much greater than usual. Up to sixty per cent sometimes. How can anyone survive on only forty per cent of their earnings? And why can the bosses get away with it?"

"This is all news to me, Peter," answered Bob. "Have the workers complained to the authorities?"

"How can they complain? If they say anything, their houses are burned down or their wives meet with unfortunate accidents. There is nothing these bad people won't do."

"Well, Peter, I assure you I will look into it. This is not something the Governor or Her Majesty would condone."

"We know that, *Bwana*, but these workers are too scared to say anything."

AS IT WAS THE SCHOOL HOLIDAYS Bob didn't have to take the children to school the next morning and so he walked to work along the path beneath the coconut palms, arriving an hour earlier than usual. He made straight for the Queen's portrait. He had not slept well. All night he had tossed and turned, worrying about what Peter had told him. Yes, it could all be exaggerated but there had to be a grain of truth in the story.

"Your Majesty," he began.

Good, she was there.

"Yes, Mr Dukes."

"Something disturbing has come to my attention. My Swahili housekeeper, Peter, told me yesterday that far from being the wonderful place we all expected the new hotel and casino to be, for the locals it is *Mahali Mbaya*."

"*Mahali Mbaya*? Mr Dukes. As you know, I speak French, but I don't speak Swahili."

"*Mbaya* means bad or unpleasant, Ma'am. The locals have made a play on words and changed the name from *Mahali Mzuri*, good place, to *Mahali Mbaya*, bad place," Bob explained to the Queen.

"Is that so terrible, Mr Dukes? It's probably just a joke."

"No, Ma'am, with all due respect. They are saying it's wicked and evil, not just bad. And the reason they give is that the workers employed by the project were and are being exploited by what they call 'the bosses', forced to hand over up to sixty per cent of their earnings to these anonymous men. If they make a complaint, unforeseen accidents happen to those concerned or to their family members."

"I see. That's not a good start to what is supposed to be a great period of expansion and prosperity for the island."

"What should I do about it, Ma'am? I don't want to cause more trouble for the workers."

"You couldn't do better than to seek the Liwali's advice. He has his ear to the ground. But do it informally," suggested the Queen.

"Thank you, Ma'am. I'll do that right away."

BOB PHONED THE LIWALI and made an arrangement to run up the north coast to see him that afternoon. The Liwali was the administrative head of the Muslim community at the coast and on the island of Mazita. It was a non-governmental appointment but an important one, as the Liwali acted as a spokesperson for the community.

As usual when visiting the Liwali's farm, he took his children with him to play with the Liwali's. Once the children were settled on the white sands of the beach in front of the Liwali's palm-thatched house, the two men could talk freely.

"What's so urgent that it can't wait, Bob?" asked the Liwali, hoisting up his long white robe or *kanzu* so that he could sit down on a small carved stool.

"I've been hearing rumors that all is not as it should be at the new hotel and casino complex of *Mahali Mzuri*," began Bob. "The locals have gone so far as to give the hotel the nickname, *Mahali Mbaya*."

"I haven't heard anything, Bob, but the workers wouldn't do that without a good reason. Do you know why?"

"They say that 'the bosses' are running a scheme where they take up to sixty per cent of the workers' wages. They enforce this with a high degree of intimidation, even going so far as to burn down houses and attack family members."

"It's interesting you should be telling me this, Bob, because I've heard similar rumors about the work force at the new cement factory at Buri. As you know, it's on the coast between Mazita and here."

"That was also built with loans from the CI Bank, wasn't it? And, of course, it has been supplying all the cement and concrete used in the construction of the new hotel/casino. Do you think there's a connection?"

"Apart from the source of the loans? No, not that I'm aware of. But I'll see what I can find out."

"Be careful," warned Bob. "If the reports are true, these are not people to trifle with."

The two men agreed to keep in touch and let each other know as soon as there was anything to report.

Chapter 5 — Investigations begin

OVER THE FOLLOWING WEEKS Bob didn't uncover anything new, nor did his discreet enquiries elicit any concrete evidence in support of the existing rumors.

The *Mahali Mzuri* had opened as planned the week before Christmas and was fully booked over the holiday period. From January through to February, the hotel continued to boom. It looked as if the decision to approve the project was leading to a bonanza on Mazita.

Then in the middle of March Sir Phillip called Bob into his office. As usual when this happened, Bob was apprehensive. The Governor's summons never boded well for Bob. What could it be this time?

"Bob, we have a touchy situation on our hands," the Governor said.

When don't we? thought Bob.

"Sir?"

"I have just been contacted by the local senior audit partner in the firm of Grantham and Jones. A Mr David Jenkins. He tells me in the strictest confidence that his firm have uncovered an irregularity in their routine audit of the cement factory at Buri."

"What does that have to do with us, Sir? Buri is on the mainland. It's in Opunto. Mazita is a separate crown protectorate."

"Yes, of course, I know that, Bob. But Mr. Jenkins says that the apparent fraud involves the *Mahali Mzuri,* or at least its construction."

"In what way, Sir?"

"I'm not that familiar with the ins and outs of auditing practice, Bob, but I understand that during a routine test of sales invoices, the auditors traced a sample of invoices back to the order and the delivery note. They turned up an invoice for eight cubic yards of concrete but the relevant delivery note was for only five cubic yards."

"And no one queried the sales invoice?" asked Bob.

"Apparently not. What does that tell you?"

"It could be one of two things: either the accounting system at the cement factory and/or the hotel site office is sloppy – this can be verified - or there is fraud going on. For that there would have to be collusion between members of the staff of the two concerns."

"Jenkins said they investigated the production records at the factory. The batch note for that delivery tallied with the delivery note at five cubic yards. It was just the sales invoice which was out of step. And so they went on to check out all the deliveries to the hotel site office and match them against the relevant sales invoices."

"Don't tell me, Sir," interrupted Bob. "The sales invoices were all inflated."

"Spot on! So what do we do? It looks as if Mazita is directly involved?"

"Let me make some phone calls and I'll get back to you, Sir."

"Make it snappy, Bob. We have to get to the bottom of this as quickly as possible. A financial scandal could ruin the reputation of Mazita as an off-shore banking center."

"Possibly, Sir. It would scare off the good money, but it might make Mazita more attractive to bad money."

"This isn't the time to be flippant, Bob," cautioned the Governor with exasperation.

"I apologize, Sir," said Bob and left to make his phone calls.

Of course, Bob asked the Queen what she thought of the situation.

"It all sounds a little too complex for me," she said. "But I've always found that when one wants something sorted one should go to the top. I think you should call in the Fraud Squad of the London Metropolitan Police."

"How do I do that, Ma'am? Opunto is an independent country. President Mzee Jefferson Jambo isn't going to take kindly to the British police marching in and ferreting about in his country's affairs."

"With the utmost tact, Mr Dukes. You have to make Mzee Jambo think that it is his idea, then he won't lose face."

"How am I going to do that, Ma'am?"

"Mr Dukes, I've told you before. You underestimate yourself. Appeal to his wish to be the foremost statesman in Africa. If that doesn't work, explain how rumors of corruption so early in his presidency could harm the gross national product of Opunto, thus appealing indirectly to his own pocket.

Then let him find the solution after suggesting it to him first."

"You really think I can do it, Ma'am?" asked Bob seeking reassurance from the Queen.

The Queen reaffirmed her belief in Bob's ability to bring about the desired end, and reminded him that she had every confidence in him as her Man in Mazita.

Bob hurried off to put the plan before the Governor.

The Governor's only modification was to suggest that Bob take the Liwali with him, as the Liwali was an Opuntan citizen and had firsthand knowledge of the goings-on at the Buri cement factory. The Governor decided that Bob and the Liwali should leave on that night's up-country train from Mazita to arrive at the Opuntan capital the next morning at eight o'clock.

In the event, it proved difficult to persuade JJ to come up with the idea of calling in the Fraud Squad. Bob did wonder about the cause of his resistance to the suggestion, but then he forgot about JJ's reluctance as he and the Liwali continued to try for the President's consent. At last, JJ seemed to realize that an investigation by the Fraud Squad was inevitable and he proposed asking the Foreign and Commonwealth office for their help.

Two members of the Squad arrived the next morning from London. They traveled down to the coast at once where they carried out a thorough investigation of the financial dealings of the Buri cement factory and of Hotel *Mahali Mzuri*. Bob was surprised to hear that their findings had then led them to continue their enquiries at the CI Bank. He wondered why.

All was revealed at a high level meeting held at Government House a week later. Those in attendance were Sir Phillip as Chairman, the Liwali, the two members of the Fraud Squad, the local senior partner of Grantham and Jones, a member of JJ's cabinet and Bob, himself.

Chief Inspector Barnes of the Fraud Squad took the floor.

"First of all, let me say that this has been one of the most difficult cases my colleague and I have ever worked as it involves a state of corruption which is both multi-faceted and multi-layered."

"What exactly do you mean by multi-faceted?" asked Sir Phillip, looking puzzled.

"Broadly speaking, it involves conspirators, if we can call them that, at the Buri cement factory and the Hotel *Mahali Mazuri*—"

"But we know that already," broke in the Governor again.

"What you didn't know, Sir, with the greatest respect, is that the CI Bank is also involved. At the heart of the matter there is a scheme in place to legitimize, or clean funds, sent to the CI Bank in Mazita in the form of large deposits. The bank then lends these funds out to businesses in Mazita."

"What's wrong with that?" asked JJ's representative.

"Well, this is the tricky bit. The businesses who borrow the money then repay it with interest to the bank. The bank holds onto the funds for a while and then wires them back to the original depositors."

"I don't see that that's a problem," said Sir Phillip.

"At first sight, no," agreed Chief Inspector Barnes. "But it all depends on the legitimacy of the source of the funds. But I'll get to that in a minute. Let me explain the multi-layered aspect."

"Please do," said Sir Phillip.

"The people behind this nefarious scheme have not been content with merely cleansing their money. They are greedy and it was their greed which led to their discovery. With the degree of separation provided by the bank in their primary scheme, we probably would not have been alerted had it not been for the secondary petty schemes which were put in place."

"Such as the invoice fiddling," said Bob beginning to understand where the Chief Inspector was going with his explanation.

"You've got it, Bob. Someone arranged for the milking of the profits of the hotel complex through the cement factory. All the extra proceeds from the inflated sales invoices have been paid out of petty cash to an unknown individual."

"Who?" barked Sir Phillip. "They should all be hanged."

"We don't know yet. We are still working on that point. Also, someone, possibly the same person, has been running an extortion racket and collecting sixty per cent of the wages of the construction workers while the building was going on, and is now doing the same with the hotel staff and the staff at the cement factory."

"It all sounds rather involved to me," said Sir Phillip. "Don't you have any idea who the culprits are, Chief Inspector?"

"Yes, we do, but we need to make further international investigations to be sure. Whispers from Interpol are telling us that there is a Mafia connection."

"What?" exploded the Governor. "You've got to be joking!"

"Not at all. We are almost certain that the funds in question are derived from the Mafia's heroin trade. We have known for some time that the American Mafia has withdrawn from the trade and passed the mantle onto the Sicilian Mafia."

"How do you know that?" asked Bob.

"There was a secret high level meeting of the American and Sicilian Mafia bosses held at the Grand Hotel des Palmes in Palermo in 1957. One of the attendees leaked the decisions of the meeting to the CIA. He's no longer alive to help us with this investigation, of course – you don't break the code of *omertà* with impunity as you know.

"However, his report of the meeting states that the Sicilian Mafia agreed to take over the smuggling of raw opium from both the Golden Triangle, and the new production areas of the Golden Crescent. Furthermore, they actually decided to set up heroin production laboratories in Sicily, in addition to the existing ones in Turkey. From these labs the Sicilian Mafia have been smuggling the heroin into the United States and Europe."

"So they have to disguise the takings from this trade, is that what you are saying?" asked the Governor.

"Exactly," answered the Chief Inspector. "And we think Mazita is one of the financial sites they have chosen to do this."

"So where do we go from here?" asked Sir Phillip. "You say you need proof? Is that right?"

"That's correct, Sir. But tell me, do you notice anything odd about this meeting?"

The Governor looked round the table in a state of bemusement.

"Of course, I've just realized," said Bob. "Why isn't Joe Nolini here? Surely he's an interested party?"

The Liwali spoke for the first time, "Perhaps too interested."

"Indeed," answered Chief Inspector Barnes. "We have our suspicions about Mr. Giuseppe Nolini, as he is Sicilian and the kingpin in the *Mahali Mzuri* development. I suggest we adjourn the meeting while my colleague and I continue with our investigation into both the Mafia connection, and Mr Giuseppe Nolini. Meanwhile, none of this must leave the room."

Everyone agreed. The meeting broke up with many expressions of astonishment and bewilderment at such a turn of events.

Bob returned to his office immediately, anxious to consult the Queen about the day's strange revelations.

"So the Fraud Squad have their suspicions about Giuseppe Nolini?" she said.

"Yes, Ma'am. It makes sense when you think about it. He is the person who arranged the deposits at the CI Bank and who set up the hotel/casino project. They just need to find and prove a definite connection between the Mafia and Nolini. It's not enough that he is Sicilian."

"It would come as no surprise to us, would it, Mr. Dukes? You've always thought there was something odd about him."

"Don't forget Charlie's reaction to him. Brand new bike aside, Charlie has always thought he was creepy, that's what he said 'creepy'."

"Out of the mouths of babes and sucklings, Mr Dukes."

"If Nolini is the guilty one, he's a bit more than creepy, Ma'am. He's a dangerous man."

"I agree. One doesn't climb to the upper echelons of the Mafia without committing at least one murder to prove one's sincerity and loyalty."

"And to think he's been around my children. It's a terrifying idea."

"You're going home for lunch now, aren't you, Mr Dukes? Why don't you tell your children that they have to stay inside the house and garden for the time being. Just to keep them safe. We don't know how tight security really is on this investigation."

Chapter 6 — Investigations Continue

THEY DIDN'T HAVE TO WAIT LONG for the next meeting. Chief Inspector Barnes called late in the evening two days later to say that he now had the desired information. Unfortunately, it was now Friday - the Sabbath Day for the Muslim members of the panel. Moreover, it was Good Friday for the Christian members. Notwithstanding religious considerations, all agreed that they had to meet. The same group re-assembled in the Governor's office to hear what the Chief Inspector had to say.

"Everyone's been helping us with this: the CIA, the FBI, Interpol and the British authorities. The FBI have uncovered the record of another interview with the Mafia squealer. In the second interview he gave a complete list of the attendees at the Palermo meeting. And, guess what?"

"What?" they all asked.

"One of the men at the Palermo meeting was a certain Giuseppe Nolini. He was a young man at the time, only twenty years old. Apparently, he was the favorite of Michele Navarro, the then boss of the Corleone family in Sicily. The meeting discussed Nolini's potential, and it was decided that he should be sent to the States under the tutelage of Joseph Bonanno, to get a financial education and some social polish. When Leggio took over from Navarro in Sicily, Giuseppe Nolini joined his team as a *capodecina*, a sort of Mafia team leader."

If Chief Inspector Barnes had expected an outcry at his news, he was disappointed because the table sat in complete silence.

Then the Governor said, "Well I never! That Nolini really is a wolf in sheep's clothing and no mistake."

"I can't say I'm surprised to hear that Nolini is a crook," said Bob. "I never did like the cut of his jib, but I would never have believed in a million years that he had ties to organized crime."

40

"And here in Mazita and Opunto," added the Liwali. "Most of my compatriots have never even heard of the Mafia."

"What's the next step, Chief Inspector?" asked the Governor.

"You will have to involve your local police force and have Nolini arrested on corruption charges. It's going to prove difficult because transferring money about the world is not against the law as such. It's only illegal if the source can be proved to be 'ill-gotten gains'. Even so, the Americans haven't managed to come up with a specific crime. The closest they can get to it is what they call 'delinquency'. I suggest you lock him up on suspicion for the allowed twenty-four hours while we work out how to handle this."

"If all else fails, can we get him for extortion and intimidation, Chief Inspector?" asked the Governor. "He could be put away for a number of years on those charges, surely?"

"That's our fall-back position, Sir. Now, once he's in the cells, I shall contact London and see what chance there is of bringing the heavier charges. But with it being Good Friday and with the Easter weekend ahead of us, it could be Tuesday before we receive the information we need."

"And this is a busy time of the year for our local police, Chief Inspector. The monsoon season has brought the dhows down from the Makran coast and Oman, and across from India. With so many dhows unloading in the old port throughout March and early April, there are always fights, disputes, smuggling charges and the odd stabbing to keep our officers working round the clock. They'll have to drop everything to deal with this Nolini business. But so be it."

The Governor wound up the meeting. Nolini was to be arrested at once. They could hold him for twenty-four hours without charging him – the *habeas corpus* rules allowed for that. The Chief Inspector would consult with London. Come Saturday evening if they were still awaiting an answer, they would go ahead and charge Nolini with intimidation and extortion, pending London's decision on the more serious crimes, stemming from his relationship with the Mafia.

They were to meet on Sunday, that would be Easter Sunday, to discuss progress.

WHEN BOB ARRIVED HOME, he gave the children an outline of what had happened. Nolini was behind bars and likely to remain there. Charlie was jubilant and the girls astounded.

"But, unfortunately, I have to go into the office for a meeting on Sunday morning," their father added.

"But, Daddy, it's Easter Sunday," complained Charlie.

"I'm sorry, children, it just can't be helped. We have to make sure that we can put Joe Nolini in prison for a long, long time. But I'll tell you what we'll do. We'll have our Easter eggs on Sunday morning at breakfast as usual and then I'll take you down to the Old Port before I go to work. You can catch the ferry boat across the creek to the swimming club, spend the morning there and then come back over on the ferry at lunchtime, and cycle home. I'll put your bikes on the roof rack as I usually do. You can leave them with the *askari* at the Customs House on the dock. How does that sound?"

"Oh goody," said Suze. "I love going across the creek in the ferry boat and this is the first chance we've had these holidays."

"But Daddy, you must tell Suze and Charlie that they are to listen to me when I tell them what to do," insisted Poppy.

"You hear that. Suze and Charlie, you are to obey your sister. She's in charge. Now why don't you go and check that your bikes are up to the trip?"

ON THE SATURDAY, Bob received a phone call from Chief Inspector Barnes to say that with the news of Nolini's arrest and detainment, employees in the accounts departments of both the cement factory and the hotel had decided to turn Queen's evidence. The case against Nolini on the minor charges was therefore sound. The Mazita Chief of Police could go ahead and charge him with extortion and intimidation.

With Nolini safely behind bars and likely to remain there for the foreseeable future, Bob and his family made the planned trip down to the Old Port on the Sunday morning.

The ferry across Samaki Creek from the Old Port to the swimming club on the northern mainland was nothing but a rowing boat. And the creek was wide and deep. Although people swam in the shallows on both sides of the creek, rumor had it that there were sharks in the deep water in the middle.

Some parents might think him irresponsible to allow his children to catch the ferry on their own but Bob knew that Poppy was sensible, and that the chances of anything happening to the children were remote. They had a large degree of freedom to roam about the island and have adventures. In fact, there were no rules except those the children established for themselves.

Moreover, they could all swim like fish. He would phone the club from his office at Government House to make sure they had arrived safely, as he usually did when they took the ferry.

Bob asked the Customs *askari* to look after the bicycles and set about finding a ferry man to row the children across the creek.

That took some time because all the workers were busy unloading the dozen or so dhows which were tied up in a double row alongside the dock.

The children loved the noisy and smelly place. It was like a trip back in time to the Arabian Nights and the adventures of Sinbad.

Poppy, Suze and Charlie were playing a game of hide and seek when their father returned with a ferry man. Once the children were seated in the boat, Bob tipped the ferry man and waved them off. The swimming club on the other side of the creek was an old low building with deep verandahs and a corrugated iron roof. Terraces planted with palm trees for shade ran down from the clubhouse to the beach. Steps led down to the pier which jutted out into the creek.

It wasn't Bob's habit to stay and watch the children crossing, but for some reason that morning he did. The rowing boat made slow progress as a slight swell ran down the creek with the incoming tide. Halfway across the boat had to stop for a while to make way for the late arrival of another dhow. Once it had passed, the ferryman took up the oars and they moved off again. When the figures in the boat were barely discernable Bob waved again, turned and walked back up to his car.

As soon as he reached his office he phoned the club to ask whether the children had arrived safely. The barman assured him Poppy, Suze and Charlie were fine; they were sitting on the verandah drinking Cokes. Bob asked the barman to call the ferry over at half past eleven to take the children back across the creek to the port. That settled, Bob put the phone down and turned round to find Nigel Flatt, the Requisitions Officer, standing behind him.

"What do you want?" Bob asked. He didn't waste any effort being friendly with Flatt. Bob didn't like the man and wondered what he was doing in the office on a Sunday morning. Snooping, probably.

"Checking up on your children, are you?" asked Flatt. "I couldn't help overhearing. They're at the swimming club, are they?"

"Yes they are – not that it's any of your business," snapped Bob. "You might knock next time before you walk into my office. Just what do you want?"

"I heard voices and thought I should check things out as I was walking past. You can't be too careful. What are you doing here on a Sunday? It must be something serious to make you give up your Easter Sunday with your family."

"Nothing much. The Old Man wants to see me, that's all," said Bob, pushing Flatt out of the doorway and locking his office behind him.

Chapter 7 – Diversion

AT ELEVEN THIRTY the barman at the swimming club picked his conch shell up off the bar, and walked down to the end of the pier to blow a summons for the ferry boat. When Poppy heard the blast, she told Suze and Charlie to collect their belongings together and make their way down to the end of the pier. But Suze was being difficult.

"I can't find my other flip flop," she said, hopping about on the hot sand.

'Really, Suze. The ferry man will be annoyed if we keep him waiting. Daddy will worry if we aren't back home in time. You've got about fifteen minutes before the boat arrives. If you can't find your flip flop by then, you'll just have to do without it."

"Don't be so mean, Poppy," said Suze, as she gingerly tested the sand with her bare foot again.

"Suze, hop up onto the pier. The wooden planks aren't as hot as the sand," her sister told her. "Charlie and I'll look for it."

It was all very well for Suze to make a fuss but they had to catch the ferry on time.

"I've found it," called out Charlie running down the steps outside the clubhouse. "You didn't look very carefully, Suze. It was under the table."

"Oh thanks, Charlie," said Suze putting it on and joining her sister to walk to the end of pier. "Come on, Charlie. The boat's nearly here."

When the ferry man bumped his rowing boat against the steps of the pier and shipped his oars, the three children were standing ready. It was a different boatman, not so friendly. Although they climbed into the boat smoothly and sat down quickly, saying "*Jambo*" to him, he ignored the children's greetings and shouted, "*Pesi, pesi.* Hurry up!" Scowling at them, he turned the boat round to point the bow out towards the Old Port.

It was nearly noon and the tropical sun baked down from directly overhead. Poppy thought the ferryman must be hot and tired and so she paid little attention to his attitude. She was more concerned that they had forgotten to bring their sunhats with them. With the reflection from the water, they would be lucky to get away with only a mild dose of sunburn.

Halfway across, Suze began to mess about, leaning right over the side of the boat to scoop up handfuls of water and splash it on her legs and arms. Charlie, as usual, copied her.

"*Chunga watoto wako!* Control those kids!" snarled the ferryman at Poppy.

Poppy was trying to, but Suze was in a silly mood.

"Sit down, you two. If you fall out of the boat here we might not be able to rescue you and there's no lifebelt."

"Oh, you're always so bossy, Poppy. We're only having fun," cheeked Suze.

"Daddy let's us use the ferry because he trusts us to be sensible. If you can't behave, I shall have to tell him, Suze."

"Oh, all right then," said Suze, sitting back down with a flounce.

This disruption had taken Poppy's attention away from their progress. They were now nearing the port. The boatman had changed course and was rowing the boat under the lee of a large dhow anchored in the outer lane. Maybe he didn't realize he was off course as he couldn't see where he was going.

"*Angalia nyuma yako*! Watch out – behind you!" she shouted. "*Jihazi! Jihazi!* You're going to bump into a dhow!"

The boatman ignored her. If anything, he put on a spurt and pulled right in under the side of the dhow, shipped his oars and caught onto the rope ladder which hung over the side. He looped the bowline through one of the rungs.

"What's happening Poppy?" asked Suze, looking puzzled.

"I don't know but I don't like the look of things," Poppy answered.

Charlie whispered, "Poppy, I'm frightened."

The boatman snapped his head round to look at them. "Shut up!" he shouted and grabbed hold of Charlie and Suze.

His shout had alerted one of the sailors on board. He climbed hastily down the ladder to take Charlie from the boatman and carry the boy up to the deck. Poppy was struggling in the rowing boat trying to pull Suze away from the boatman, but he hit her hard across the face with his free hand, knocking her back down into the well.

While she scrabbled about trying to find her feet in the rocking boat, the ferry man climbed up the ladder, dragging Suze with him. As he reached the top, the sailor started back down the ladder to get Poppy.

"Oh no, you don't!" she said and dove over the side into the sea. She swam underwater away from the dhow for a good thirty yards towards the shore, next to the port before she came up for air.

She crawled out of the sea under cover of a low cement wall which ran down from the fish market into the water. She peered cautiously round the end of the wall but there was no one on the deck of the dhow. Suze and Charlie had obviously already been taken down below.

Poppy's first thought was to hide and evade the inevitable pursuit. She crept along behind the wall until it fetched up at the rear of the fish market. There were some large metal waste containers there. Perhaps she could hide in the space between the containers and the wall. They smelt strongly of rotting fish but she would have to put up with that. Moving as quietly and quickly as she could, she darted into the space only to be brought up short. Right in front of her, sitting propped up against the wall, was the first ferry man.

His blank open-eyed stare and the blood congealing on his ragged shirt told her he was dead.

She had no idea what happening. All she knew was that she had to hide for now and then fetch help for Suze and Charlie when it was safe to do so. Taking a deep breath, she willed the panic away. She had to think clearly now, of all times. Her thoughts cleared. It wasn't a good hiding place anyway. She had to find another one. She remembered that people didn't look above their heads. She glanced around and noticed a tall Indian almond tree growing on a piece of waste ground between the fish market and the building next door.

Checking round quickly to make sure no one was looking, she ran lightly over to the tree and climbed up into the branches. As well as being out of sight in the tree, she had an excellent view of the old port and of the dhow where Charlie and Suze were being held.

Poppy lent back against a branch and wrung the water out of her skirt. It was too far to walk home and she couldn't fetch her bicycle because she couldn't risk being seen crossing the open space to the Customs House.

No sooner had she made the decision to stay
hidden in the tree than she saw a group of
sailors burst out onto the deck of the dhow she
was watching. Amid much calling and shouting
in Arabic and Swahili, they climbed over onto
the deck of the dhow alongside the dock and
then ran down the gangplank. They fanned out
and began searching the area. They had to be
asking the dock workers if they had seen
Poppy.

Two of the men started to walk towards her
tree. Poppy kept as still as possible as she
observed their progress. They had seen her!
But no, they were sneaking off for a quiet
cigarette in the shade. Poppy heard them say
that it was much too hot to be rushing about
looking for child who had probably drowned
anyway.

A whistle blew and the men looked up.
"Praise be to Allah!" they said and drifted back
to the dhow.

The port gradually shut down for the long
tropical lunch period. Poppy settled down to
wait.

CHAPTER 8 — REACTION

THE MEETING AT GOVERNMENT HOUSE ran on until one o'clock and so Bob didn't return home for lunch until half past. He was immediately alarmed to find that the children were not home when he arrived. Their bicycles weren't there and so they hadn't returned and then gone out again somewhere. Even allowing for a puncture, they should have been home half an hour earlier. Bob didn't know if anyone had phoned. There would have been no one to take a message because it was Sunday, Peter's day-off. He called the swimming club and learned that the children had left on the return journey across the creek at a quarter to twelve.

His first thought was to trace the route the children usually took back from the Old Port and then make enquiries at the Port if he hadn't come across them on the way. He was just getting back into his car when a police Land Rover came speeding down the drive and stopped in a swirl of dust beside him.

It was the Chief of Police.

"Bob, I'm afraid there has been a new development."

Bob felt a kick in the solar plexus. He knew at once something untoward had happened to his children.

"What's happened?"

"We've just received an anonymous phone call demanding that Nolini be set free and put on a chartered plane, together with a bag containing all the foreign currency available at the local banks."

"Oh no, don't tell me. They've got my children."

"I'm afraid so. If we don't comply, your children will be killed or sold as white slaves."

"Did they give us a deadline?" asked Bob.

"We bargained for midday tomorrow. Ostensibly to give us time to collect the cash together, but the real reason was to give us a chance to find the children. We can't trust the kidnappers to give them back alive even if we do meet Nolini's demands."

"I was just on my way to look for them. I dropped them at the Old Port this morning. They were to make their own way home on their bicycles. We had better check there first and see if anyone saw anything."

"Right, get in my car and we'll collect some of my *askaris* on the way. It's better if we all arrive together. If you go on your own you might scare the kidnappers into doing something rash."

UP IN THE INDIAN ALMOND TREE, Poppy was dozing off. It was the lunch period when work stops on the Equator. The dock workers and sailors were all asleep wherever they could find a spot of shade. The only creature moving was a *shenzi* dog scavaging about down by the dock.

It was the put-puttering of the engine of the police launch which woke her. Poppy watched it patrolling slowly along the lines of dhows. It was the Governor's escort launch from Government House. That had to mean that her father had organized a search for them.

She peered out of the branches, but didn't dare come out of her hiding place while the only help was out there on the sea.

Then she heard police sirens. Coming round the corner at the top of the road leading down to the Old Port was a police Land Rover, all lights flashing. It was accompanied by two police vans. The vehicles stopped abruptly. Doors flew open. Khaki and blue uniforms spread out to left and right, enclosing the fish market and the Customs House. Her father was there with the Chief of Police.

Poppy climbed halfway down the tree and jumped the rest of the way.

"Daddy! Daddy!"she called as she ran across the concrete to the gates and her father's open arms.

"Oh Poppy, I'm so glad to see you're all right," he said. "But where are Suze and Charlie?" Without waiting for a reply, he turned to the Chief of Police. "You don't think the kidnappers have killed them, do you?"

"No, I don't think they would risk murder right here in the Old Port –" began the Chief Inspector.

Poppy interrupted, "They killed the ferry man. I found his body behind the fish market."

"Why didn't you tell us that straight away, Poppy?" asked her father.

"I haven't had time," she said, bursting into tears. "I'm awfully tired and hungry. I feel so bad because I was supposed to be in charge, and now Suze and Charlie are in great danger. All because of me."

Bob pulled his daughter to him and hugged her again. "Poppy, it's not your fault. This is a grown-up situation caused by an evil man. You've done brilliantly for a girl of twelve."

When she stopped crying, Poppy explained what had happened. Suze and Charlie were being held prisoner on one of the dhows, she said, and she showed them which one.

"Let's hope we're in time," said her father.

The Chief of Police took some of his men and boarded the dhow at once. They carried out a thorough search of the boat. But no Suze and Charlie.

The Chief called Poppy over and took her on board to see if she could identify the two men who had been involved in their capture, but the men in question were nowhere to be seen.

A complete search of the dock area and the other dhows yielded nothing. No one knew anything.

"The kidnappers must have moved Suze and Charlie on somewhere else at some point when Poppy couldn't see them because she was dozing, or because they were out of sight behind the dhows," said the Chief of Police.

"There's nothing more we can do here today," he added. "I suggest you take Poppy home, Bob. My staff and I will continue with our investigations. We may turn something up which will lead us to Suze and Charlie."

Bob collected the children's bicycles from the Customs House and drove home. Both Poppy and her father were at a loose end all afternoon. They were too anxious to settle at anything. In the end Bob took Poppy and the three dogs for a long walk along the beach and back.

He sent Poppy to bed early telling her she had had a taxing day and needed the sleep. He rang the Chief of Police for a bulletin but there was no news.

POPPY COULDN'T SLEEP. She was worried about Charlie and Suze. She was positive they were concealed down at the Old Port somewhere. She was sure she would have noticed any disturbance during the quiet lunchtime period. She still felt guilty about being unable to prevent their capture or secure their rescue. She just had to put things right.

At ten o'clock Poppy heard her father go to bed. She gave him half an hour to fall asleep. Then she crept out of bed, down the steps to the ground level and collected her bicycle from the shed. Fortunately, the dogs were spending the night outside and she was able to stroke them and reassure them so they didn't gambol about barking.

She cycled down to the Old Port, stopping before she reached the gates and stowing her bicycle away out of sight. Scrambling over the low wall she made her way to the Indian almond tree again. It was still the best look-out around. She climbed up into the branches and sat to wait to see if anything moved.

The dock workers had all gone home long ago and all was quiet and still. Now and then a burst of shouting bounced up from one of the dhows which were moving gently to and fro at anchor, their red and green riding lights scribing small circles of light in the moonless black of the night.

The *shenzi* dog appeared out of the shadows and came trotting along the dock and across the port concourse as he snuffled about for scraps of fish. He came right up to Poppy's tree. She froze not daring to breathe lest she set him off barking. But he wasn't interested in Poppy. He cocked his leg. Having left his mark, he disappeared rapidly in the direction of the Old Town.

Poppy watched and waited.

Chapter 9 — Time for Action

CHARLIE AND SUZE WERE TIRED AND HUNGRY, too. This was the tenth hour of their captivity. The two men who had hauled them on board had dragged them down to the bottom of the ship. Every time the children asked why they were there and why they were being treated that way, the men shook them roughly and told them to be quiet.

They spoke angrily to each other about the repercussions of Poppy's escape and took their annoyance out on the children. They gagged them and tied their hands and feet, taking little account of their age. Then the men opened a disguised wooden bulwark in the stern of the ship and thrust the children inside.

When the police search party came on board, the children heard them and their eyes brightened only to dim again when the footsteps and voices retreated. Imprisoned in the secret locker and bound and gagged, they couldn't call out or bang on the wall to attract attention.

Charlie couldn't hold out any longer; he burst into tears. He had been brave up to that point. Being the only man present, he had been strong for his sister but now he felt helpless. And he desperately needed to pee and Suze did, too. With hands and feet tied together there was nothing they could do but let go and wet themselves.

When one of the Arab crewmen opened the hatch after nightfall, the two children were huddled together in their damp clothes, fast asleep on the wooden planks.

The clunk of a lantern being placed on the floor woke them both. They levered themselves into a sitting position and stared wide-eyed at their jailer.

"For the love of Allah, this is no way to treat children," he said clucking his tongue. "And such pretty children!"

He took a curved dagger from his waistband and cut Suze's bonds, leaving her to pull off her gag while he attended to Charlie.

"Why are we here?" she asked. "You must be bad men to do this to us."

"I don't know why you are here, little one. All I know is, I have orders to keep you locked up."

"Does our Daddy know we are here?" asked Charlie.

"Yes, he does."

"I don't believe you. He would come and fetch us if he knew," said Charlie with defiance.

"He knows you are our prisoners but he doesn't know where you are exactly," said the man. "Your father has to give the big boss something before he can have you back."

"What?" asked Charlie and Suze together.

"Stop asking questions, you silly children, and eat the food I've brought you," said the sailor reaching behind him for a cooking pot he had placed on the floor outside the locker. "Here, eat and drink. Then go back to sleep."

Suze and Charlie were starving. They dipped their hands into the pot at once to scoop up the rice and meat. The light shining on the pot wavered. Suze looked up to see the sailor backing out of the locker with the lantern in his hand.

"Oh no!" she wailed. "Please don't take the light. I am so afraid of the dark."

Charlie added his entreaty, "My sister has to have a light at night. If you let us keep the lantern, I will tell the Chief of Police you have been kind to us when he rescues us."

The sailor laughed, "Very well, my little blond prince. You may keep the lantern."

He put it on the floor and left, locking the door behind him.

Suze looked at Charlie. "Thanks Charlie," she said. "I'll never tease you again. I promise. Let's eat everything up in case they don't give us any more food. We don't know how long we are going to be here."

"I've been thinking about that," said Charlie through a mouthful of rice. "Daddy's not going to look for us here because they've already searched the boat and they didn't find us."

"So what can we do?" asked Suze.

"Finish eating and then we'll explore and see if we can find something we can use to break the lock."

Once the cooking pot was empty the two children started examining the locker carefully. It was like being inside a wooden crate. The walls were the crudely hewn planks of the inside of the hull. The floor and ceiling were the wooden decks above and below. They couldn't find anything of any use nor could they find any openings. But they did find a row of old plywood tea chests, one of which was open.

"Help me take the lid off, Charlie. There might be something inside we could use," said Suze.

They took the lid off and lent it against the hull. Inside the box there were rows of brown paper packets about the size of a bag of flour.

"What's this? asked Suze trying to pull the corner off one of the packets. "Have you got something we can cut it open with?"

"How about my belt buckle?" asked Charlie, taking his belt off and handing it to Suze.

Suze jabbed the buckle spike into the packet and made a small slit.

"It's icing sugar!" said Charlie. "Bags and bags of icing sugar. How peculiar!"

Suze wet her finger and dipped it in the sugar. "It doesn't taste like sugar," she said licking her finger.

"What do you think you're doing?" shouted an angry voice from behind them. They hadn't heard the hatch open. The once friendly crewman was crouched in the doorway.

"Nothing," said Charlie, dropping the lid back on the tea chest.

"Don't touch that! It's poisonous. Come. I'm taking you to a cabin on the deck above. Captain's orders."

The cabin was a great improvement. A mattress lay on the floor – tatty but more comfortable than the wooden planks. The air was fresher as there small square portholes at head height. Charlie's face light up when he noticed them.

"What is it, Charlie?" Suze whispered.

"Shush!" he warned, indicating the sailor with a slight nod.

"Here, catch!" said the sailor, throwing a couple of shirts at the children. Charlie put down the lantern and caught them. The shirts were clean but old and faded. "Put those on. The captain doesn't want dirty children in his cabin," he added, as he left and locked the door behind him.

Charlie listened at the door until he was sure the man had left then he turned to Suze. "I've got an idea."

"I hope it's a good one. I'm scared. No one is ever going to find us here. Something terrible is going to happen to us. Do you think they are going to kill us?"

"They wouldn't dare," Charlie assured his sister.

"What's your idea then?"

"We could flash the lantern out of the porthole and try and attract someone's attention," said Charlie. I thought of it before - that's why I asked for the lantern - but there wasn't a porthole at the bottom of the ship."

"I don't think anyone will take any notice of another flashing light. There are flashing lights all over the place. On the light buoys. On the dhows.

"I know," said Charlie. "We could try doing that special code – you know the one with dots and dashes. They use it in war films. The only thing is, I can't remember how it works."

"Charlie, you're so clever. And I know what the code is. It's *'S O S'*. We learned it at Brownies. It's *'dot dot dot, dash dash dash, dot dot dot'*. It's easy to remember because it's all in three's."

"Let's do it then. See if you can find a piece of cardboard or something, to hold up in front of the lantern."

"Will this do?" Suze held up a copy of the local newspaper she had found lying on the floor.

"That's perfect," answered her brother.

They decided that Suze would hold the lantern as she was the stronger, and Charlie would flash the folded newspaper in front of the light in time to the signal. They would do it five times and then stop for a few minutes before starting all over again.

POPPY JERKED SUDDENLY. She had just caught herself drifting off to sleep. It had been an eventful day. Oh, how she wished she had noticed what the ferry man was doing before it had been too late. They could all have escaped into the sea and swum for it, if she had realized what was happening before he had grabbed hold of Charlie and Suze.

She looked out over the creek, searching for movement. All was motionless except for the gentle rise and fall of the dhows. As she turned to glance behind her at the Old Town, a blinking light caught her attention. Then it flashed a few times. Then it started blinking again. Then a pause.

It was shining out from the dhow where Charlie and Suze had disappeared. A yellow light, not one of the red and green riding lights. There it was again. Blink, blink, blink, flash, flash, flash, blink, blink, blink.

Could it be a signal? Poppy was sleepy and cold. She watched the light for a minute or two before the rhythm sank in. It was definitely a signal ... it was '*SOS*'! It had to be Charlie and Suze. Now she knew they were still being kept prisoner on the dhow the police had searched, she must get help at once.

She jumped down from the tree, picked up her bicycle and rode home as fast as she could.

WITH POPPY'S REPORT of where the children were being held relayed to him by Bob, it didn't take the Chief of Police long to have Suze and Charlie set free. They were soon home with their father and older sister. Bathed and well-fed they went to bed, still a little frightened, but overall none the worse for their adventure.

Chapter 10 — More than one Way to skin a Cat

NEXT MORNING the interested parties met at Government house again. The hoped for advice had arrived by telex from the Foreign and Commonwealth Office. It had been confirmed that Nolini and his accomplices could not be charged with the more serious offences. Furthermore, the Governor had been instructed that Nolini was not to be charged with extortion and intimidation either. It was considered that the publicity from these charges would be just as damaging to the future of Mazita as the charges of complicity with the Mafia.

"How about the heroin which was found on the dhow?" asked an angry Bob Dukes. "Can't we get him for that? We can't let him off everything. He kidnapped my children, for heaven's sake."

"We can't prove that he had anything to do with the kidnapping or with the heroin smuggling at this stage, Bob. The best we can do there is charge the captain and the crew of the dhow," answered the Chief of Police.

"Is that really all we can do?"

"We could discharge Nolini tonight and re-arrest him immediately on the smuggling and kidnapping charges. That would give us another twenty-four hours to come up with some proof," the Governor suggested.

Then he instructed the Chief of Police to do that and to put pressure on the captain and crew of the dhow to see if they could be persuaded to implicate Nolini.

Bob had to be content with that for the time being.

He called into his office before he returned home to his children. He wanted to speak to his friend, the Queen.

"Mr Dukes," she said. "As this is Easter weekend I haven't had a briefing from my government for a few days now. All this is news to me. However, I am sure that my Government was acting in the best interests of the country as a whole when they advised the Governor to drop all the charges against Giuseppe Nolini.”

“But Ma’am. He’s a dangerous crook and he kidnapped my children and threatened to kill them. He shouldn’t be at large. He should be punished for what he has done.”

Just then the internal phone rang. It was the Governor to say that the captain of the dhow had decided to turn Queen’s evidence, and give up Nolini.

“There you are, Mr Dukes. Giuseppe Nolini stands the chance of being found guilty of kidnapping at the very least now. But what I don’t quite follow is how did Nolini know that the children would be using the ferry yesterday.”

“That’s easy to explain. That nasty piece of work, Nigel Flatt, heard me phoning the swimming club. He’s the only one who could have passed the information on. The Chief Inspector is going to pull him in for questioning and he’s sure to confess to save his own skin when he finds out that the dhow captain has already done so.”

"You look exhausted, Mr Dukes. Why don't you go home to your children now and let the police bring all the guilty parties to justice?"

BUT THAT WAS NOT TO BE. No sooner had Bob reached his house than the children came running down the steps to say that the Governor was on the line and wanted to speak with him urgently.

"What now?" Bob asked.

The Governor was calling to say that once again HM's Government had intervened. They had the same reservations about charging Nolini with smuggling and kidnapping as they had had for the crimes of extortion and intimidation. Too much adverse publicity for the new off-shore center of Mazita. The charges were just too sensational.

"I'm sorry children, I have to go back to the office for a short while," Bob said, turning round to find three apprehensive faces waiting to hear what the Governor had said.

Back at the office, Bob went straight to his office to confer with Her Majesty. He had found that whenever he had a difficult problem to resolve, the Queen would either have a solution, or she would shake up his own ideas and lead him to one himself.

"Oh dear, Mr Dukes," she said when she heard the latest twist in the story. "Perhaps we are just going to have to settle for deportation and ship the rotter off to be someone else's headache."

"I was hoping you would be able to think of something, Ma'am. You usually do."

The Queen sighed and closed her eyes. "It is so challenging when everyone expects one to be able to smooth things over all the time."

Bob waited hopefully. Her Majesty had never let him down yet.

After a couple of minutes of deep thought, she opened her eyes again slowly. "Mr Dukes, who is the most famous Mafia character you can think of?"

"Al Capone," Bob answered without hesitation.

"Right, Mr Dukes. Now what happened to him?" the Queen asked.

"He was eventually caught, tried and locked up, Ma,am. But I don't see how that helps us here."

"Mr Dukes, Don't you remember? Al Capone was never tried for his evil and murderous Mafia career – he was charged and found guilty of tax evasion."

"I see where you're going, Ma'am, but we don't have any taxes in Mazita. It's an off-shore financial center."

"Mr Dukes, sometimes I despair of you. Don't look at the detail, look at the method. Go and find some lesser crime with which to charge him. One which will ensure that he has to go to prison, but which will not be so sensational that my Government objects to it."

"Ma'am, that's a brilliant idea. I'll go and see the Chief Inspector at once and see what he can come up with."

LATER, BOB WAS BACK to tell the Queen what had happened. The Chief of Police had remembered that he had come across Nolini's name once before.

Nolini had been caught poaching lobster with Mr Dominque LaGrange, his cousin's father-in-law. Apparently, Nolini and LaGrange had made a habit of going out in a small boat and picking up spiny lobsters from the shallows, using an underwater light as a lure. At the time the two men had been let off with a caution as it was thought to be a first offence.

The Chief of Police had called LaGrange in for questioning again. He had confessed to a substantial trade in illegally caught lobsters and had implicated Nolini as his partner in crime.

"Got him!" said the Queen.

"But Ma'am, the longest possible sentence is only five years. That's hardly commensurate with the enormity of his crimes."

"Don't you worry about that, Mr Dukes. For a member of the *Cosa Nostra* the greatest misfortune that can befall him is the loss of his Mafia honor. I can see the headlines now –

"GIUSEPPE NOLINI

THE LOBSTER MOBSTER

"Who's going to take him seriously with an epithet like that?" said the Queen. Then she added, "That's if he lives to tell the tale, of course!"

THE END

Note from Katie Penryn

I hope you have enjoyed reading about Bob Dukes and his three children, Poppy, Suze and Charlie. If so, please consider leaving a review on the site where you purchased this book. You can access this and my other books through my website.

On my website you can sign up for my newsletter about new stories and/or special offers:

http://www.KatiePenryn.com

I love to hear from my readers and answer all emails personally:

KatiePenryn@gmail.com.

The other stories in the *Our Man in Mazita* series are:

Beau—ootiful Soo—oop!

Something Spotted

Christmas in Mazita

You can purchase these through my website.

HAVE A HAPPY DAY!

Notes:

Notes:

www.ingramcontent.com/pod-product-compliance
Lightning Source LLC
Chambersburg PA
CBHW071458030726
47593CB00003B/1050